Enid Blyton's
Twelfth Bedtime Book

By the same author

Enid Blyton

Twelfth Bedtime Book

DRAGON
Granada Publishing

Dragon Books
Granada Publishing Ltd
8 Grafton Street, London W1X 3LA

Published by Dragon Books 1984

First published as *Enid Blyton's Eleventh
Bedside Book* by Arthur Barker Ltd 1959

ISBN 0-583-30674-8

Printed and bound in Great Britain by
Collins, Glasgow

Set in Times

Contents

THE BIG GIRL

Whenever little Jane went down to play on the beach she saw the Big Girl.

She always called her the Big Girl because she didn't know her name, and she was tall and rather proud-looking. Little Jane was rather afraid of her, although she liked the look of her very much.

She did her best to get the Big Girl to notice her. She walked near her, but the Big Girl didn't even look her way. She ran by the Big Girl very fast indeed, hoping to hear her say,

'Dear me – how fast that little girl runs!' But she didn't take any notice at all.

Another time, Jane saw that the Big Girl had gone paddling and had left her shoes rather too near the edge of the sea. So Jane ran to move them a little farther back. But the Big Girl wasn't pleased.

'My shoes were quite safe,' she said. 'Please don't move them again.'

And then when the Big Girl was lying on the beach, half asleep, her newspaper blew away. Jane was after it at once! She caught it and took it back to the Big Girl.

SHE CAUGHT IT AND TOOK IT BACK.

'Thanks,' said the Big Girl. 'But you needn't have bothered. I've read it.'

After that Jane gave up. She didn't try to make the Big Girl notice her any more. But she still liked her and thought she could swim wonderfully well, and row beautifully, and run like the wind. 'She's just the kind of girl I'd like for a friend, if only I wasn't small and she wasn't so big,' said Jane to herself.

Now one morning Jane was by herself on the beach. The sea had covered up the sand, and there was only a stretch of shingle left. Nobody can make good castles with stones, so Jane thought she would do a little shell-hunting.

'I'll take a beautiful collection of shells back home with me,' she thought. 'Then I can look at them and remember the sea.'

So she began to hunt for shells. She found some winkle shells and cockle shells. She found some limpet shells, shaped like little pointed hats. Jane thought those were really very pretty.

She found a big scallop shell, shaped like the sunset rays of the sun. That was lovely.

And then she found the prettiest little shells she had ever seen! They were small, cone-shaped, and the brightest greeny-blue imaginable. Jane had never seen any like them before, except some that were glued on to the top of Granny's old work-box.

'But they are even prettier than those,' thought Jane. 'And not a bit broken. Quite, quite perfect!'

She hunted about that bit of shingle for a long time, and found forty-one little shells there, all alike, and all perfect. She couldn't believe her luck. She hunted in another spot, too, but she couldn't find any more of the shells. She looked at them in delight.

'They're fairy-shells,' she said. 'Much, much nicer than any of the others I've found.'

THE BIG GIRL WAS CRYING.

She stood up to go home, her forty-one precious shells in her small bucket, and the other shells in her big bucket. She set off over the beach.

She suddenly saw the Big Girl quite near her – and, good gracious, she was crying! Jane stood and stared at her. Wasn't she too big to cry? And whatever could she be crying about? Had someone been unkind to her?

Jane went up to her. 'Please,' she said, 'is anything the matter? Why are you crying?'

'Oh – hullo,' said the Big Girl hastily dabbing her eyes with her hanky. 'Nothing's the matter, really. I've lost something, that's all. I know I'll never find it on this beach, but I think I must have lost it here.'

'What have you lost?' asked Jane.

'My very prettiest necklace, the one I liked the best of all, that my mother gave me,' said the Big Girl, and tears came into her eyes again. 'I hate losing things. I'm a real baby when I lose anything. But it *was* such a pretty necklace.'

Jane hated losing things, too. She felt very sorry for the Big Girl, and wondered what she could do to make her feel better. Then she suddenly remembered something. She would give her the forty-one beautiful shells! She held out her bucket.

'You can have my shells,' she said. 'My nicest ones.'

The Big Girl smiled through her tears. She looked down into the little bucket. 'Oh no – I don't want . . .' she began, and then she gave a little squeal.

'Oh! OH! Where did you get them? Why, they're mine!'

Jane was astonished. 'No. They're not yours. I found them.'

'Listen! The necklace I lost was a *shell* necklace!' cried the Big Girl. 'It was made of little, teeny-weeny, blue-green, shiny shells like these. *Just* like these. Did you find all these shells together?'

'Yes, I did,' said Jane. 'Oh, your necklace must have broken just there – and all the little shells fell in one place. And now, I do remember, there was a little green thread there, too – that must have been what the shells were threaded on! I wonder if I've picked up every single one?'

'There should be forty-one,' said the Big Girl. 'Oh, I say – what a bit of luck! Oh, I do feel pleased. And to think you were sorry for me and came up to give me my own shells that you liked so much. I think you must be very nice. What's your name?'

'Jane,' said Jane, delighted. 'What's yours?'

'Margaret,' said the Big Girl, and Jane at once thought that was the nicest name she had ever heard. 'Will you come to tea with me this afternoon? Shall we go for a bathe together first?'

Jane's face was one big beaming smile. Now she had the Big Girl for a friend. How lucky she was!

The Big Girl was pleased, too. This little Jane was nice. She had never had a small sister. Jane would make a very good one!

And now you can see them with one another every day, having fine times together. You'll know the Big Girl by her shell necklace – it's still as pretty as ever.

PEOPLE

I'd like to meet old Santa Claus,
And peep inside his sack,
And ride upon his reindeer sleigh,
All the way and back!

I'd like to meet old Puss-in-Boots,
And Jack and Jill as well,
And Humpty-Dumpty on the wall –
I'd catch him when he fell!

I'D LOVE TO MEET

But most of all I'd like to meet
Brer Rabbit, sly and funny,
I'm sure he'd play a trick on me,
That clever old Brer Bunny!

I wouldn't mind – I'd laugh and laugh,
And give his ribs a poke,
And tell him that I love him best
Of all the story folk!

LITTLE HARRY'S MILK

THERE was once a very small boy called Harry who didn't feel well. So he called his mother and said, 'Mother, I'm not well. I think some good fresh milk would do me good. Please do get me a glassful! There's a cow in the field over there. Maybe she would give me some.'

So his mother took a mug and she ran out to the cow. 'Please, cow, give me some milk for Harry!' she begged.

But the cow shook her tail and said: 'Madam, I have just been milked. Go to the farmer and maybe he will dip your mug into a pail of my good warm milk!'

So the mother went across the field and through the gate till she came to the farm.

There she saw the farmer walking in his yard. She called to him.

'Please, farmer, give me some milk.'

But the farmer shook his head and said: 'Madam, I have just taken all my cow's milk and put it into a big churn. And the churn I have put by the roadside for the lorry-man to pick up and take to the station. Hurry and see if you can catch him.'

So the mother ran to see the lorry-man, and she found him in the lane, driving his big milk-lorry. She called to him, 'Please, lorry-man, give me some milk!'

But the lorry-man shook his head and said: 'Madam, I've just been to the station and left the milk-churns there. Hurry and ask the station-master to let you have some milk.'

'PLEASE, FARMER, GIVE ME SOME MILK.'

Then the mother ran to the station and saw the station-master. 'Please, station-master, give me some milk for Harry,' she said. But the man shook his head and said: 'Madam, it's gone by train to town. Here comes another train. Hop in and maybe you'll catch the milk.'

So she hopped in and her train followed the milk-train. When she came to town, she ran to a porter standing on the platform, and she called to him: 'Please, porter, give me some milk!'

But the porter shook his head and said: 'Madam, I have just sent the churns to the big dairy. Go there and maybe you will get the milk.'

So the mother went to the dairy, and when she got there she spoke to the girl behind the counter. 'Please, dairy-maid, give me some milk for Harry.'

Then the girl took the mug and poured it full of rich, creamy milk. 'Madam, this has come straight from the cow,' she said. 'It is this morning's good fresh milk!'

'I know!' said the mother. 'I had such a chase to get it!' She took the milk and went out. She went to the station and saw the porter. 'I've got the milk,' she said. She hopped on the train and soon came to her village. She waved to the station-master. 'I've got the milk,' she said. She walked through the lane and she passed the lorry-man. She held up the mug of milk to him. 'I've got the milk!' she said.

She saw the farmer and she called to him. 'I've got the milk!' And then she came to the cow, lying down in the field, chewing the cud. 'I've got the milk!' she said.

She came to her home, and there was Harry, patiently waiting. 'I've got your milk!' cried his mother. 'Drink it up and you'll soon be well! You've no idea what a story there is in a cup of milk, Harry!' And she told him this story just as you will tell it to your little brother or sister!

RIDDLE-ME-REE

My first is in Game but not in Win,
My second's in Peg, but not in Pin,
My third is in Bird, but not in Beast,
My fourth is in Most, but not in Least,
My fifth is in Piglet, and also in Pig,
My sixth is in Large, but not in Big,
My seventh's in Day, but not in Night,
My eighth is in Snarl, but not in Bite,
My last is in Den, but not in Lair,
My whole is something that flies in the air.
What am I?

Answer on page 32

HE TAUGHT HIMSELF A LESSON

'SHUT the door after you, Miggy!' shouted old Mr Tumps. But Miggy had gone, and Mr Tumps had to get up and shut the door himself.

'That careless little goblin!' he grumbled. 'Never wipes his feet – never shuts a door – never puts anything back in its right place!'

Not very long after that Miggy was being shouted at again, this time by old Dame Rickety. 'Wipe your feet, Miggy – you go right back to the front door and wipe your feet! *Look* at the mess you've made with your muddy shoes all across my kitchen floor!'

Miggy sulked. 'Bother! I'm always being told to shut doors and wipe my feet! How fussy people are! As if my feet were as dirty as all that!'

They *were* dirty. They couldn't help being dirty because Miggy always walked in the very muddiest places, and never once cleaned his shoes. He didn't wash his hands much, either, and always left dirty marks on walls and doors. He really was a dirty little grub.

But once he taught himself such a lesson! People in Teatime Village, where he lived, often longed to teach Miggy a sharp lesson, but somehow they never could. And then one day he taught himself a lesson he never forgot.

He went down Muddy Lane, treading as usual in the very muddiest places, and splashing even his trousers with mud! He was on his way home, thinking of the muffins he would toast for his tea.

Then he remembered that he had broken his toasting-fork. Bother, bother, bother! Now he would burn his hands when he tried to toast the muffins.

He came to a little crooked cottage. It belonged to Dame Sharp-Tongue. Miggy was afraid of her – but he wasn't afraid of little Jemima, her servant.

'I'll go round to the kitchen door, and ask Jemima to lend me Dame Sharp-Tongue's toasting-fork,' he thought. So round to the back door he went.

But nobody answered his knock, which wasn't surprising because there was nobody in. Miggy knocked again – rapitty-tap.

'Nobody at home,' he said. 'Well – I'll see if the door is locked.'

He turned the handle and the door opened! In he went. Did he wipe his dirty, muddy feet? No, of course not! Down the nice clean hall he went, leaving big muddy footmarks behind him, and into Jemima's beautifully clean kitchen. He left the trail of his dirty hands on the wall. He left patches of mud on the clean, newly-scrubbed kitchen floor. He took the toasting-fork and smile joyfully.

'Now I can toast my muffins for tea!' he said, and went down the hall again and out of the door. Did he shut the door behind him? Of course not! Miggy never shut a door unless somebody shouted at him.

Now, when Jemima came back, she brought crumpets for Dame Sharp-Tongue's tea, and, of course, she meant to toast them well. The first thing she noticed when she got home was that the back door was wide open.

'Look at that!' said Jemima. 'Who's been here and left my door wide open, making the house as cold as ice? IS ANYBODY HERE?'

Nobody was – but a minute later Dame Sharp-Tongue came back too, and Jemima heard her coming in at the front door. 'Get my tea, Jemima,' she called, 'and toast those crumpets well!'

Jemima was staring in horror at her floor. My goodness me, look at all those muddy footmarks! WHO had been walking up and down her nice clean hall, and WHO had been right across her kitchen to the fireplace and back? What had been taken?

She soon knew when she went to get the toasting-fork for Dame Sharp-Tongue's tea. 'There's no toasting-fork!' she cried in dismay. 'Somebody has been here and stolen Dame Sharp-Tongue's beautiful brass fork. Dame, Dame – there's been a robber here!'

'Who?' asked Dame Sharp-Tongue, running into the kitchen.

THEY LOOKED IN AT THE LIGHTED WINDOW AND THERE WAS MIGGY.

'I don't know,' said Jemima. 'He's taken your best toasting-fork, the one you got from the Magician High-Hat. Who *can* the thief be?'

Dame Sharp-Tongue looked at the floor and saw the muddy footmarks.

'Ho!' she said, 'there's only one person in Teatime Village who could leave *those* marks behind! Did he leave the door open behind him, too?'

'Yes, he did, Mistress,' said Jemima. 'Oh – of course – it must be Miggy. The rascal, the rogue!'

'Come along – we'll soon see if it is,' said Dame Sharp-Tongue, and she and Jemima hurried down the lane to Miggy's untidy cottage. They looked in at the lighted window – and, sure enough, there was Miggy, still wearing his muddy shoes, toasting his muffins with Dame Sharp-Tongue's best toasting-fork.

The old dame went into the cottage like a whirlwind and almost frightened Miggy out of his skin.

'How dare you go to my house and steal my toasting-fork?' she shouted.

Miggy was dreadfully scared.

'I didn't,' he stammered. 'S-s-somebody – lent it to me!'

The old Dame took him by the collar and bent his nose over the floor. 'See those marks,

Miggy? They are all over *my* kitchen floor too! And my door was left open. Who does things like that but you? Aha, Miggy, now you're going to be punished! I'm going to put you on the end of my toasting-fork and toast *you*!'

Miggy squealed and got away. He ran out of the door. He ran and he ran and he ran. What – be toasted on a fork by Dame Sharp-Tongue? Never!

He ran right into the old duck-pond in the dark, and what a mess he was when he waded out! He crept back to his cottage, glad to see that nobody was there. He had to have a bath and wash all his clothes. He was hungry because he had had no tea. He was very sorry for himself indeed. He shivered because a draught blew round him. 'Bother! I've left the door open!' he said, and went to shut it. Then he sat down in his old dressing-gown by the fire and thought very hard.

'If I'd wiped my feet and remembered to shut the door at Dame Sharp-Tongue's I wouldn't have been found out,' he thought. 'I'm silly – and I'm bad. People keep saying they'll teach me a lesson – but I've taught myself one instead. I'll be different now. I DO hope Dame Sharp-Tongue won't remember that she meant to toast me in front of the fire on her long toasting-fork!'

Dame Sharp-Tongue was surprised to see Miggy at her door the next day. He had come to say he was sorry, and to beg her not to toast him.

'Well – if *you* remember to mind your manners, and to wipe your feet, keep your hands clean and shut doors behind you, *I'll* remember not to toast you on my fork,' said Dame Sharp-Tongue, with a twinkle in her eye. 'But if you forget, Miggy – just BEWARE!'

He won't forget. He's much too afraid of that long toasting-fork – though, of course, Dame Sharp-Tongue wouldn't really toast him!

Who Stole the Bun?

Who stole the bun?
Not I, said the cat,
I was here on the mat.

Not I, said the pup,
For I wasn't up.
Not I, said the horse,
Though I'd like it, of course!

Not I, said the goat,
It would stick in my throat!

Not I, said the duck,
I hadn't the luck!
Not I, said the goose,
For I wasn't loose.

Then WHO stole that bun?

I think it was Joe,
For I saw him go
Off like an arrow that's shot from a bow!
But alas, down he fell,
And the bun went as well,
And where it has gone to
I really can't tell!

UMBRELLAS FOR THE DOLLS

ONCE Aunt Twinkle asked the dolls' house dolls out to tea with her and her nephews, Pip and Jinky. She liked them very much, for they were small and dainty, and had beautiful manners.

'You and Jinky can look after them at tea-time,' she said to Pip. 'And just see that your manners are as good as theirs! Remember, too, not to help yourselves to the cake until everyone else has a slice.'

'But there might not be any left then,' said Pip, in alarm.

'That's just exactly why I said you're not to help yourselves,' said his aunt. 'Visitors must always come first.'

Well, the dolls' house dolls came. They were just about as big as Pip and Jinky, and they all had on their very best clothes, and looked perfectly sweet.

It was a wonderful tea, and there was plenty of cake for everyone after all. They played games after tea, and then it was time to go home.

'Oh, dear!' said one of the little dolls in dismay. 'It's pouring with rain. Our best party dresses will be spoilt.'

'I haven't enough umbrellas for you all,' said Aunt Twinkle, worried. 'Pip – Jinky – think of something quickly!'

'Half a minute!' cried Pip, and he ran out into the rain. He went to where the primrose plants grew. He had often noticed that the rain ran off their crinkly leaves – they were as good as umbrellas, those leaves! The primroses liked them crinkled because then the rain trickled off down the crinkles, and the plant itself didn't get soaked.

Pip picked twelve leaves and ran back. 'Here you are – fine green umbrellas for each of you!' he cried. 'Look at their crinkles – the rain will run down them and you won't get a drop on your pretty clothes!'

He was right. The dolls' house dolls went home safely and arrived quite dry, each hold-

'HERE YOU ARE – FINE GREEN UMBRELLAS FOR EACH OF YOU!'

ing a primrose leaf umbrella over her head. As for Pip, he and Jinky had an extra slice of cake each – they *were* pleased!

ANSWER TO RIDDLE-ME-REE
Aeroplane.

THE EXTRAORDINARY CHAIR

THERE was a dear little toy chair in the playroom. All the toys could sit in it nicely. It was a bit tight for the fat teddy bear, and a bit big for the clockwork mouse, but most of the toy animals and all the dolls could sit down in it very comfortably.

And then Bertie, the Boy Doll, came to live in the playroom. He belonged to Pat, the little girl whose playroom it was, and when he first came, she showed him to all the toys.

'This is Bertie, my new Boy Doll,' she said. 'I've had him for my birthday. I want you to be nice and friendly to him, please.'

So, of course, all the toys *were* nice and friendly. But Bertie wasn't nice and friendly to them! He took all the best things for himself.

'I want to sleep in that big cot,' he said to Juliana, the curly-haired doll. 'So you must make room for me too. And I want a special corner in the toy cupboard. And dear me – what a very nice chair that is – I'll have that for my own, to sit in when I'm tired.'

Now the little chair was a great favourite with the toys because it was soft and comfortable, and they all sat in it in turn. It was a wicker chair, just like the one Pat's Mummy had in her bedroom. It had no legs, but had wickerwork all round the bottom, and was nicely padded inside.

The toys were very cross with the Boy Doll. 'It's most rude of you to sit so much in our chair – you have had far too long a turn in it,' they said. Bertie was lazy and liked to sit down nearly all the time.

Well, of course, as soon as he knew it

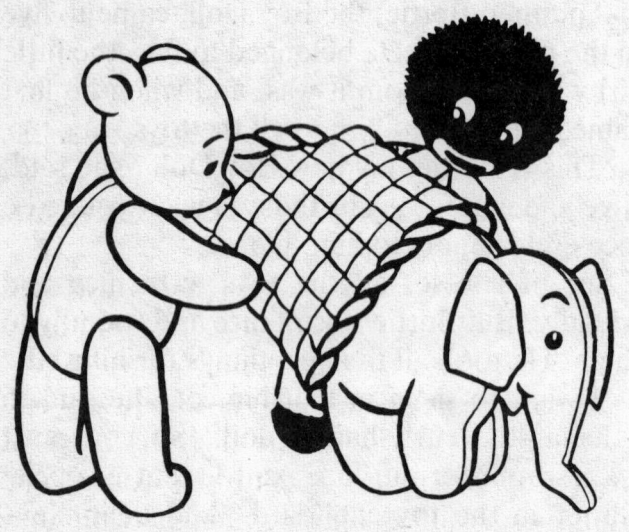

THEY LIFTED UP THE WICKER CHAIR AND THEN PLACED IT CAREFULLY OVER JUMMY.

annoyed the toys to see him sitting so much in their favourite chair, he sat in it all day long! Nobody could move him out because he was big and strong. What a nuisance!

And then Jummy, the little toy elephant, had a grand idea. He called the toys round him. 'I say! You know that there is a space under the bottom of the wicker chair seat, don't you?' he said. 'It's hidden by the wicker-work that goes round the bottom of the chair. What about me getting in that hollow space and playing tricks with the chair?'

'Oooh yes,' said Juliana. 'Could you make it jig about and slip away from Bertie when he goes to sit in it, Jummy?'

Everyone giggled. '*That* would scare him,' said the teddy bear. 'Let's put you under the chair now, Jummy, because Bertie has gone out for a walk with Pat. Let's see if you fit into the space beneath.'

So they lifted the wicker chair and then placed it carefully over Jummy. It was rather a tight fit but never mind!

And then the chair began to do most peculiar things! It slid along the floor by itself. It jigged up and down. It turned round and round and round! The toys laughed till they cried!

It was Jummy, the little toy elephant under

the chair, who was doing it all, of course! He was walking and jigging and turning round and round under the chair, carrying it with him. But *he* couldn't be seen. It looked very queer and funny indeed.

'Sh! Here comes Bertie,' said the teddy bear, suddenly. In came Pat with Bertie. She put him down on a doll's cot and left the room. Bertie leapt off the cot and went over to the chair.

'I'm tired after my walk,' he said. 'I'll have to sit down.'

He sat down. The toys watched him. Would Bertie be too heavy for Jummy to move the chair when he was in it? Still, Jummy was very strong. After all, he was an elephant!

The chair slid along the floor a little. Bertie looked alarmed. He set his feet firmly down to stop the chair sliding about.

Jummy jigged up and down under it, and the chair hopped about a little.

Bertie caught hold of the wicker arms in surprise. The clockwork mouse couldn't help letting out a little squeal of laughter.

The chair stayed still for a while and Bertie felt better. But then Jummy began to turn himself round and round, and the chair went too, of course – and so did Bertie! He clutched the arms in fright.

'What's happening, what's happening? The chair's gone mad! Help, help!'

'It doesn't like you,' cried the teddy bear, doubling up with laughter. 'Get out, Bertie, it doesn't like you!'

Bertie leapt out. The chair at once stood absolutely still. The toys roared with laughter at Bertie's face.

'This is silly,' said Bertie. 'A chair can't like or dislike anyone. The floor must be slippery or something.'

'Better leave that chair alone, Bertie,' said the golly. 'It might run off with you!'

'Pooh!' said Bertie and sat down bump, in the chair. It kept quite still. 'There you are!' said Bertie. 'It's quite all right now. Go away, all of you. I want a nap!'

He shut his eyes. Soon he gave a little snore. 'He's asleep, Jummy,' whispered Juliana. 'Do something.'

Jummy did! He suddenly ran at top speed to the door, and the chair went with him, of course! Bertie woke up with a yell, clutching the arms of the chair in fright. What was happening now?

'The chair's running away with you, Bertie! It will tip you down the stairs!' shouted the toys. 'Look out, look out, it's nearly there!'

But Bertie didn't get out in time, and when

BERTIE WAS TIPPED RIGHT OUT!

Jummy, still under the chair, came to the top of the stairs he stopped so suddenly that Bertie was tipped right out! He rolled bumpity-bump down the stairs from the top to the bottom! The chair fled back to the playroom.

'Take the chair off me, quick, before he comes back!' begged Jummy the elephant. 'I'm feeling dreadfully squashed. I don't somehow think Bertie will EVER sit in our chair again!'

The teddy bear lifted the wicker chair off the little elephant, laughing till the tears ran down his cheeks. The chair stood still on the floor, and didn't move after that. Bertie came creeping back into the nursery, frightened and bruised.

'Poor Bertie!' said Juliana, with a squeal of laughter. 'You look tired and frightened. Have a sit down in your chair!'

Bertie shivered. 'I'm never, NEVER going to sit in that extraordinary chair again,' he said. 'Never. You're right – it doesn't like me. Horrible thing! Anyone can have it now – *I* don't want it!'

And after that he never sat in the little wicker chair again. As for the chair, it hasn't behaved in such a peculiar manner since that exciting day – but oh, how I *wish* I'd been there when it all happened!

CRAWLER THE TORTOISE

Ronald was very cross because he had lost the bright new sixpence that his Uncle Fred had given him the day before.

'I must have dropped it somewhere in the garden,' he said to Annie, his sister. 'Perhaps it is on the lawn, where we played ball yesterday. Will you help me to look?'

So Annie and Ronald hunted on the grass, where Crawler, Annie's tortoise, watched them out of his bright little eyes. Ronald was running to what he thought was his bright sixpence, when he tripped over the tortoise, and fell down, bang! He hurt his knee and was very angry with Crawler. He gave the tortoise such a smack that he put his head back in his shell at once, startled.

'Don't, Ronald!' cried Annie. 'It was *your* fault you fell, not Crawler's. You should have looked where you were going. You're not to smack the poor old tortoise.'

Ronald smacked Crawler again. 'I don't like your tortoise,' he said. 'Silly, slow creature, just good for nothing! Making me fall over like that!'

Annie was angry. She took Crawler away from Ronald and wouldn't help him to look

HE HURT HIS KNEE AND WAS VERY ANGRY WITH CRAWLER.

for his lost sixpence any more. So Ronald didn't find it and was very sad.

That day Crawler disappeared! Annie felt certain Ronald had hidden him, but Ronald said he hadn't touched him at all. Annie hunted all over the garden, but the tortoise was quite gone.

'He's gone because you were unkind to him,' said Annie, almost in tears, for she was fond of her slow old tortoise. 'I think you are a horrid boy.'

Ronald was feeling ashamed of himself. He liked Crawler really, and was sorry he had gone. He made up his mind to hunt for him, and see if he could find him for Annie.

But no matter where he looked he couldn't see him! And then he remembered that tortoises bury themselves when it gets cold, and as there had been a frost the night before he thought perhaps Crawler had been afraid of freezing, and had hurried to bury himself somewhere.

So he looked carefully in the beds for any freshly-turned earth – and after a time he came to a rose-bed that looked a bit bumpy, as if someone had dug up the earth and buried something there!

He took a stick and carefully and gently poked it in the soil to see if Crawler was there.

The stick came against something hard. 'It must be Crawler!' thought Ronald in excitement.

And so it was! Very gently Ronald scraped away the earth and took the tortoise out of the wet muddy soil. Crawler wriggled feebly. He was almost in his winter sleep. Ronald carried him to Annie.

'Look, here's your tortoise!' he said. 'He was buried in the muddy earth. You'll have to clean him, Annie, and put him in his winter-box. I'm sorry I was horrid to him yesterday.'

RONALD TOOK THE TORTOISE OUT OF THE WET MUDDY SOIL.

'Oh, thank you, Ronald!' cried Annie, joyfully, and she wiped the mud off the tortoise. Something fell to the floor with a clink. It was Ronald's sixpence! Crawler had buried himself where the sixpence had been dropped and it had stuck to him in the mud! He had brought it back to Ronald!

'Oh, good old Crawler!' said Ronald, in delight. 'If I hadn't been sorry and gone to look for you I wouldn't have found my sixpence again! I'll buy you a nice bit of flannel to make you a blanket for your winter sleep!'

CHRISTMAS IS COMING

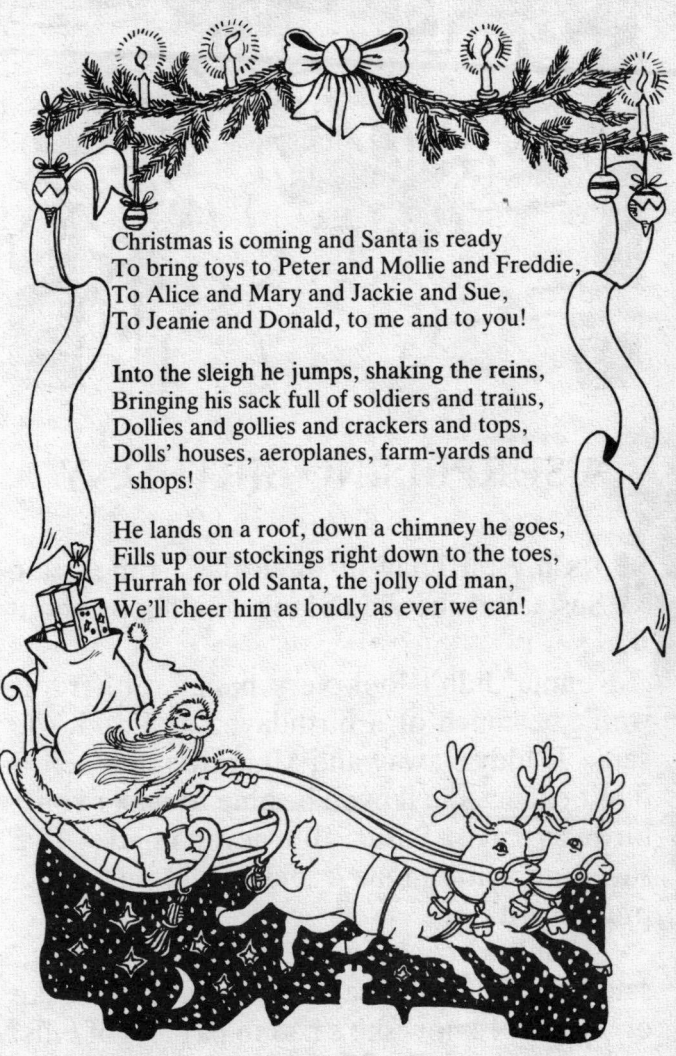

Christmas is coming and Santa is ready
To bring toys to Peter and Mollie and Freddie,
To Alice and Mary and Jackie and Sue,
To Jeanie and Donald, to me and to you!

Into the sleigh he jumps, shaking the reins,
Bringing his sack full of soldiers and trains,
Dollies and gollies and crackers and tops,
Dolls' houses, aeroplanes, farm-yards and
  shops!

He lands on a roof, down a chimney he goes,
Fills up our stockings right down to the toes,
Hurrah for old Santa, the jolly old man,
We'll cheer him as loudly as ever we can!

A SURPRISING BIRTHDAY

'I T's my birthday in three days' time,' said Susie, but she didn't look very happy about it.

Ronnie didn't look very happy, either. 'It won't be much of a birthday, I'm afraid,' he said. 'Daddy's away and Mummy's not well. I don't expect she'll even be able to make you a birthday cake, Susie. But never mind – I've saved up some money, and I shall buy you a present with it.'

'I shan't worry Mummy about my birthday,' said Susie. 'I shan't say anything about a cake or a party. I know she's had to pay lots of bills, too, so she won't have much money for a present. You tell her not to bother about my birthday this year, Ronnie.'

It was easy to say that, but it was very hard to think that she might have to miss out one of her precious birthdays. They came only once a year, and they took a very long time coming!

'It will be dreadful to miss one,' thought Susie, 'but I mustn't cry about it when my birthday comes, because no little girl should cry on her birthday.'

Ronnie told his mother not to bother about Susie's birthday that year. 'You don't feel well,' he said, 'and you haven't much money to spend, I know, so Susie says we won't bother about her birthday this year. Anyway, Daddy isn't here to share it, either.'

'Poor, good little Susie!' said Mummy. 'I do wish I could buy her a really nice present and make her a beautiful cake. I've knitted her a scarf, but that's all the present I can give her.'

Ronnie knew that Susie didn't like wearing a scarf, but of course he didn't say so. He wished he had more than a shilling to spend on Susie. A shilling wouldn't buy much. What he would have liked to buy was a big doll in the toy shop that could stand on its own feet and say 'Mam-ma' when a string was pulled in its neck.

HE WOULD HAVE LIKED TO BUY THE BIG DOLL.

Susie's birthday came. She woke up early and tried not to feel excited because, after all, a birthday that wasn't going to have proper presents or a party wasn't *really* a birthday at all.

All the same, she couldn't help feeling just a tiny bit excited. She was a year older for one thing, so she felt more important.

Mummy gave her the scarf she had knitted and Susie thanked her very much, although she did hate to feel a scarf round her neck. Still, it was a very pretty one, with red and blue stripes.

'Here's my present, Susie, but I wish I could have given you that lovely doll,' said Ronnie, and he gave Susie a jigsaw puzzle.

Susie had one card from a friend of hers, but that was all. After looking at the card and having her two presents, the day went off just like any other day. Susie couldn't help feeling that it was a dreadful waste of a birthday.

She and Ronnie went to school. They came home to lunch. They went to school again – and really, by that time Susie had forgotten it was her birthday at all! And then, when they got home at four o'clock, things began to happen!

There came a thundering knock at the door – and who should be there but Daddy! Yes, actually their Daddy, come home after a long voyage on his ship!

'I didn't think I'd get home for Susie's birthday, but I've managed it!' he said.

'What are all those parcels?' cried Ronnie.

'Presents for everybody – but most are for my birthday girl!' said Daddy. 'Many happy returns, Susie! Am I in time for a piece of birthday cake?'

'Susie isn't having one,' said Ronnie. 'Mummy hasn't been well, so we told her not to bother about Susie's birthday.'

'Well, well, well – we've got to bother now

I'm home!' said Daddy. 'Go off to the cake shop and buy a big iced cake, Ronnie – and buy eight candles to put on it for Susie. And here is ten shillings for yourself. Buy whatever you like!'

Well, you can guess what Ronnie bought! He bought Susie the doll that could stand up on its feet and say 'Mam-ma'! He brought home a beautiful iced cake, too, and eight candles with little holders to stick on the cake.

Daddy had brought a silk shawl for Mummy, a fine ship for Ronnie, and three lovely things for Susie because it was her birthday. She had a pair of red slippers, a little man who nodded his head, and a lovely blue plate for herself.

So they all had a glorious time, and sat round the tea-table happily. The candles burned on the cake and Susie squeezed Daddy's hand and smiled at Mummy, who seemed much better already, now that Daddy was home.

'I thought I wasn't going to have a birthday – but I had a lovely one after all!' Susie said. 'The nicest I've ever had! I shall remember it always.'

Hidden Animals

I have hidden an animal in each of these sentences for you. I will tell you the first one, so that you will know how to look for the others. The first sentence has APE hidden in it – you will find the word in the two words 'a pen.' Now guess the rest:

1. Shall I lend you A PEn?
2. That boy knows how to be artful.
3. I saw her at school.
4. You had better go at once.
5. Will he land safely, do you think?
6. Oh look, Jack, all my sums are right.
7. I can't eat Eric's share too.
8. Do not use all the drawing paper.

Answers on page 55

A LITTLE MISTAKE

'OH, dear!' said Aunt Twinkle, as she looked at her empty larder, 'whatever can we have for dinner today? Ah, I know! Oxtail soup! Yes, that will be delicious.'

She put 'Oxtail' down on her shopping list. Then she called to Pip. 'Pip! Stop doing that jigsaw puzzle and fetch some shopping for me. Listen – this is what you have to buy.'

Pip listened with half an ear. Then he sighed, pulled on his pixie-cap and went to the door. 'Don't you want the list?' called Aunt Twinkle, but he shook his head.

'No,' he said. 'I can remember the things. Anyway, I always lose your lists!'

He had to get sugar, a newspaper, two pots of jam, and the oxtail for making the soup. He repeated them as he ran to the shops. 'Sugar, paper, jam, oxtail.'

He bought the sugar, got the paper, and fetched the jam. Now – what was the last thing?

'Oh, dear – was it sheeptail? Cowtail? Calf-tail? Pigtail?'

'Hallo, Pip!' said a voice, and there was Jinky, his friend. 'What are you muttering

HE POINTED TO THE HAZEL TREE HEDGE.

about? Pigtails? Surely you are not going to wear your hair in pigtails?'

'Don't be silly,' said Pip, crossly. 'Aunt Twinkle told me to get some tail or other – sheeptail, would it be?'

'Oh, *I* know what she wants,' said Jinky, at once, and he pointed to the hazel tree hedge where hundreds of lamb's-tail catkins were dancing in the wind. '*Lamb's*-tails of course! She's very fond of them, isn't she? She likes to put them into a vase.'

'Yes! It must have been lamb's-tails,' said Pip, pleased, and he picked a dozen twigs with dancing catkins on them.

He took the shopping home. 'Sugar!' he said to Aunt Twinkle, putting it down on the table. 'Your newspaper. Two pots of jam – and the lamb's-tails!'

Aunt Twinkle stared at the catkins. '*Lamb's*-tails! How can I make soup with

those, silly? Now you'll have to go without your dinner. I said OXTAIL!'

Oh, dear – poor Pip had no dinner that day. All the same, the lamb's-tail catkins looked lovely on his mantelpiece! You get some for yourself in springtime, and see how pretty they are.

ANSWERS TO HIDDEN ANIMALS

1. Ape. 2. Bear. 3. Rat. 4. Goat. 5. Eland. 6. Jackal. 7. Ant-Eater. The word Hare is there too! 8. Seal.

The Water

I saw a water baby
Sitting by a pool,
Her feet were in the water
To keep them wet and cool.

A ribbon made of seaweed
Around her waist she tied,
Just like a sash she made it,
It was so nice and wide

Baby

She made herself a necklace
Of seashells from the sand,
And earrings out of cockles,
She really did look grand!

But when she saw me peeping,
She gave a little squeal,
And slipped into the water –
But I *know* that she was real!

THE CAT DID IT!

CAROLINE was cuddling the cat. It wasn't a very old cat, only just over a year, and it still had kittenish ways. Caroline loved Paddy-Paws, and Paddy loved Caroline.

Harry loved Paddy-Paws, too. He liked to chase him all over the room, and play hide-and-seek. Paddy played very well indeed.

'He hides under the bed and waits till we come by – then he pounces out on our feet.' Harry told his mother. 'He plays just like we do.'

'Yesterday he leapt up on to the mantel-piece,' said Caroline. 'And he walked daintily all among your ornaments there, Mummy – and never moved one of them!'

'Then he is cleverer than you are,' said Mummy. 'If I ask you to dust a room for me you always seem to break something! As for Harry, he's even clumsier than you are!'

Caroline looked sulky. 'I don't break much,' she said.

'Only a jug on Monday, a cup on Tuesday, a doll on Wednesday, and the jam pot yesterday!' said Mummy. 'I'm just wondering what you're going to break today. I'm afraid you will have to pay for the next breakage yourself, out of your pocket money. If you have to spend all your savings you may be a bit more careful – as careful as Paddy-Paws!'

'Are you going to make Harry pay for *his* next breakage, too?' said Caroline. 'It wouldn't be fair only to make *me* do that and not Harry.'

'Both of you will have to pay for your breakages,' said Mummy. 'So now, just be careful!'

For a whole day both children were very careful indeed. Then something dreadful happened.

They were playing with Paddy-Paws, who was chasing about all over the room. Caroline and Harry suddenly made a dart at him, bumped together and fell over laughing. They knocked against a little table and over it went. CRASH! The plant pot that stood on the top fell to the ground. The pot broke into a dozen pieces, and the plant and the soil were scattered on the carpet.

The children got up at once, frightened.

'Look,' said Caroline in a whisper, 'the pot's broken. We would have to pay about fifteen shillings for a new one.'

'We can't possibly,' said Harry, in dismay. 'I'm saving up for a railway signal.'

Mummy came running in. 'What was that? Oh, dear, oh, dear – my lovely plant – and the

THE POT BROKE INTO A DOZEN PIECES.

60

CAROLINE THREW A BALL AND IT KNOCKED A CLOCK OFF
THE MANTELPIECE.

pot smashed too. Which of you did that?'

Neither of the children said a word. Paddy-Paws came sidling up, and Harry suddenly had an idea.

'It was the cat,' he said.

'Yes,' said Caroline. 'The cat did it.'

'Naughty Paddy!' said Mummy, in such an angry voice that the cat ran off at once. The children helped to clear up the mess in silence.

The next day another dreadful thing happened. Caroline threw a ball at Harry and it knocked a clock off the mantelpiece. CRASH!

And, oh, dear, as soon as Mummy came running in to see what the noise was, what do you suppose Caroline said?

'Mummy, the cat did it!'

Mummy believed her of course. She looked round for Paddy-Paws, but he wasn't there. 'Run off scared, I suppose,' said Mummy. 'Really, it's too bad of Paddy! First the plant pot, and now a clock.'

Two days later Harry slid along the polished hall at top speed, though Mummy had often asked him not to. He lost his balance and crashed into a little table. One of Daddy's ashtrays leapt off it and smashed on the polished floor!

Before Mummy could come to see what had happened Harry rushed into the sitting-room. 'Mummy, the ashtray in the hall is smashed. The cat did it!'

Mummy was very cross. She cleared up the bits and looked for Paddy. But the cat wasn't there.

'I can't possibly let this sort of thing go on,' said Mummy, firmly. 'Paddy will have to be taught a lesson.'

Now the next day, when the children came home from school, Caroline had a little ping-pong ball for Paddy to play with. She had felt ashamed of blaming so many things on to the cat, and so she had bought him a little present. She called him.

'Paddy – Paddy – Paddy-Paws! Where are you? I've got something for you. Paddy – Paddy-Paws!'

Paddy didn't come. The two children hunted for him everywhere. They went into the kitchen, too, calling loudly.

'He's gone,' said Jane, the cook. 'Didn't you know? The dustman took him. He's got mice and wants a cat. So your Ma gave him away.'

Harry and Caroline stared in horror. They couldn't at first say a single word.

'HE'S GONE,' SAID JANE, THE COOK.

'Given away Paddy – our dear little cat?' cried Caroline, at last. 'I don't believe it!'

'Come and ask Mother,' said Harry, so off they rushed.

'Mummy – Jane says you've given Paddy-Paws away to the dustman!' cried Caroline. 'You haven't, have you?'

'Yes, dear, I have,' said Mummy. 'I couldn't possibly keep a cat that broke so many things. When I heard how badly the dustman wanted a cat for his mice, I was pleased. Paddy will

CAROLINE BURST INTO TEARS.

enjoy himself catching mice, and the dustman and his children will love him.'

Caroline burst into tears. Harry almost did, too. They could hardly believe that Paddy was gone.

'Mummy, you shouldn't have done it,' wailed Caroline. 'He didn't deserve to be punished like that.'

'Oh, yes, he did,' said Mummy. 'I told you I couldn't possibly let him go on breaking things. He'll be so busy catching mice now that he won't have time to break anything at all.'

'Yes, but Mummy – you don't understand,' said Harry. 'You don't! He never broke a thing – not one – he was the best and carefullest cat that ever lived. It was Caroline and I who broke those things.'

'And we said it was the cat,' wept poor Caroline. 'Just to save ourselves we said it was the cat.'

'And now you've punished him, instead of us,' said Harry. 'Can we go and get him back? We'll empty our money-boxes for you and pay for everything.'

'No,' said Mummy, looking very solemn. 'Certainly not. Money won't pay for all that naughtiness of yours. Giving up what is in your money-box isn't the right punishment for telling such dreadful untruths and making me blame poor Paddy-Paws. You don't deserve to have a nice cat like that. He must stay with the dustman and his family.'

She went out of the room and shut the door. Caroline cried bitterly, and Harry went and looked out of the window, very miserable. He was ashamed of himself, and so was Caroline. Paddy-Paws was bearing their punishment – he had been given away to strangers.

'Caroline,' said Harry at last. 'Let's do all we can to show Mummy we're sorry – let's empty our boxes and buy what we can – and

CAROLINE CRIED BITTERLY, AND HARRY WENT AND LOOKED OUT OF THE WINDOW.

perhaps in a few days she'll let us ask for Paddy back again.'

So they spent all their money on a new plant pot and a new ashtray. They hadn't enough for a new clock. They were as good as gold, and so kind and helpful that their mother was really astonished.

When she said they could go and ask for Paddy-Paws back again, they were overjoyed. They rushed off together to the neat little house where the dustman lived with his three jolly children.

But will you believe it, Paddy didn't seem to know them any more! He sat on the lap of the oldest child, purring loudly, but he wouldn't even look at the two children who had once owned him.

'He doesn't want to come back,' said Caroline, sadly. 'He's forgotten us.'

'He likes being here,' said Nora, the oldest child. 'He catches so many mice. We love him. And he loves us. We don't want to part with him now.'

So Harry and Caroline went home without Paddy. Mother felt sorry for them.

'I was afraid he wouldn't want to come back with you,' she said.

'I expect he thinks those other children are nicer than we are,' said Caroline.

'They'd *never* say "the cat did it" when they broke anything,' said Harry. 'They love Paddy too much.'

'Now, listen,' said Mummy. 'You've been silly and you've been sorry. Now be sensible. I'll get you another little cat if you'll never be so silly again. I'll give you a month to show me if you're good and sensible or not.'

The month's almost up – and though they don't know it yet, Harry and Caroline are going to have another little cat at the weekend. Won't they be pleased!

HE SAT ON THE LAP OF THE OLDEST CHILD PURRING LOUDLY.

THE TIRESOME TWINS

'Can we go shopping for you, Mother?' asked Daisy.

'Yes, if you'll go straight to the shops and back, and not stop here and there on the way,' said Mother. 'Last time I sent you to the grocer's you were gone two hours and I had to come and look for you.'

'We'll be very quick today,' said Dan.

Mother began to think what she wanted from the shops. 'I don't really want very much,' she said. 'Take this note to the dairy and wait for what they give you. And buy me some darning needles at the wool shop. And a rubber at the newsagent's. Here's the money. Now, it's not a long list, so you should be very, very quick.'

They took the basket and set off. They went to the dairy first and gave in the note. They didn't know that the note asked for a big block of ice cream for pudding! The girl put a packet into their basket, and took the money from Dan. Then they set off for the wool shop and the newsagent's. They bought the needles and the rubber and turned to go home.

Some men were digging up the road with a big drill. The twins stayed to watch for quite a

THEY STOPPED ON THE BRIDGE TO SEE IF THEY COULD SPY ANY FISH IN THE WATER BELOW.

'YOU'VE BEEN SUCH A LONG TIME THAT THE ICE CREAM HAS MELTED.'

long time. Then they met Hilda and Tom, who had a new bicycle and both twins wanted to try it. That took quite a long time too.

Then they stopped on the bridge to see if they could spy any fish in the water below. So, when they reached home, it was quite late!

'What *have* you been doing?' said Mother. 'I thought you were never coming!'

Daisy gave her the basket. Mother picked up the packet of ice cream, and groaned. 'Just what I thought! You've been such a long time that the ice cream has melted. Look at it dripping out of the corner of the box! What *silly* children you are! I planned to give it to you for pudding – and now you will have to

71

have the prunes left over from yesterday instead. This ice cream is no good – unless you want to drink it!'

'We didn't know it was ice cream!' said Dan in dismay. 'Oh, WHY didn't we hurry, as we said we would?'

FOXGLOVE MAGIC

'A RE we going to the seaside, Mummy?' asked Jenny. 'Like we do every year?'

'I don't think so. Not this year,' said Mummy. 'You see, everything is so *very* expensive now, Jenny – and you've grown so much I've had to buy all new clothes for you – and railway fares are so high – and we really haven't enough money to pay for rooms by the sea.'

Jenny was bitterly disappointed. But she didn't grumble. She knew that her mother ought to go away for a rest because she worked so hard. She knew that Daddy loved going out in a boat to fish and had been looking forward to it all the summer. Now nobody could go.

But it wasn't anybody's fault really. She couldn't help growing out of her clothes. Daddy couldn't help everything being so expensive.

'There's just nothing to be done about it,' thought Jenny. 'Except wish and wish – but wishes don't often come true.'

Then she thought of something. 'I'll go and look for a pixie or a goblin down in Wishing Corner. People say it is called that because fairies once did live there – and maybe there are one or two left – you just never know.'

So she went to Wishing Corner – and will you believe it, she saw a pixie there! At first she thought the pixie was just a very pretty little doll, and then she saw her run away to hide!

'Don't go away. Do come here,' called Jenny. 'I badly want to ask you something.'

AT FIRST SHE THOUGHT THE PIXIE WAS JUST A VERY PRETTY LITTLE DOLL.

'What?' asked the pixie, peeping out from behind a tall foxglove. She thought Jenny had a nice face, so she wasn't afraid of her.

'I wondered if you could give me a wish,' said Jenny. 'It's rather a big wish, I'm afraid, a wish for three people to have a nice summer holiday.'

The pixie came out from behind the foxglove. She held a tiny wand in her hand. She showed it to Jenny.

'This is the biggest wand I've got,' she said. 'And it will only grant a very little wish, I'm afraid. Not a big one like yours.'

'How else can I get a big wish?' asked Jenny.

'Well – if you could find half a dozen four-leaved clovers you might get a fairly big wish,' said the pixie.

'Oh, dear,' said Jenny. 'I've hunted so often for four-leaved clovers and I've never found more than one. I'd never find six at once.'

'No. I don't suppose you would,' said the pixie. 'Even I never have. Well, I don't know what to suggest, then. There's no wishing-well near here, or you could call down that.'

'Do you know anyone who would lend me a wishing-cap?' asked Jenny, hopefully.

The pixie shook her tiny head. 'No. I only know one person who has a wishing-cap, and that's my old uncle, Jinky-Top. But his cap is so old that its magic is almost worn out. Anyhow, it wouldn't fit you. You're too big.'

'Oh, dear – what a pity!' said Jenny. 'It did seem so lucky to meet a pixie when I badly wanted a wish to come true – and now you're no use at all!'

The wind blew and the big foxglove shook in the breeze. One of its finger-shaped flowers fell off just beside the pixie.

She gave a little squeal. 'Oh, I know! There is old, old magic in every foxglove. Foxglove is short for folk's glove, you know. We used to

ONE OF ITS FLOWERS FELL OFF JUST BESIDE THE PIXIE.

wear these fallen pink flowers on our thumbs when we wanted a wish. Why shouldn't *you* try that?'

'Well, I could!' said Jenny, excitedly. 'Of course I could. What do I do? Just slip a fallen flower over my thumb?'

'Yes – but there's more to it than that,' said the pixie. 'Wait a minute now – let me think. To begin with I'm not sure that one foxglove flower would be enough for a big wish. You'd have to put one on *each* thumb to get double magic.'

'I could easily do that – look!' cried Jenny, and she picked up two fallen foxglove flowers and slipped one on each thumb. 'Now what do I do – wish?'

'Well, if you want really strong wishing-magic, it's best to follow the old rules,' said the pixie. 'I'm trying to remember them.'

She frowned till tiny wrinkles came on her forehead. Jenny waited anxiously. Would she remember the old rules?

'Yes. I remember them now,' said the pixie. 'If you want a big wish, you have to wear a foxglove flower on your thumb every night for a week – a fallen one, of course. The ones still on the foxglove aren't magic at all.'

'Yes – go on,' said Jenny.

'And for all that week you mustn't think an

'NOW WHAT DO I DO – WISH?'

unkind thought or do an unkind deed,' said the pixie. 'I think that's why people don't use foxglove magic any more, because there are hardly any people who could go a whole week like that. I know I couldn't!'

'Well,' said Jenny. 'I could try, couldn't I? The wish isn't so much for myself, really, as for my father and mother, and I could try much harder if it's for them, than I could just for myself.'

'I see. You love them,' said the pixie. 'Well, they say that love is the biggest, strongest thing in all the world, so I suppose it would act

78

like magic in your case, especially if you wore a foxglove flower each night. All the same, you'll probably find yourself thinking a little tiny unkind thought without knowing it, I'm sure.'

'Oh, I do hope not,' said Jenny. 'I don't *think* I'm an unkind person. I love birds and animals and people. I do get cross sometimes, though. I'll have to be very careful. Oh, pixie, thank you. You've made me feel quite hopeful.'

'Please don't hope too much,' said the pixie, running between the tall grasses. 'I don't think

'PLEASE DON'T HOPE TOO MUCH,' SAID THE PIXIE,
RUNNING BETWEEN THE TALL GRASSES.

anyone's been able to use foxglove magic for at least a hundred years!'

She disappeared behind a tree. Jenny stared at the tall foxgloves round about, her eyes shining. She had seen a pixie. She had learnt a bit of old, old magic. So foxgloves were really *folk's* gloves – and the little folk used to slip them on their hands when they wanted a wish!

'And I can do the same,' thought Jenny. 'But I *must* remember about not thinking or doing anything unkind. Will it be so difficult? I really and truly don't think I'm an unkind person. Not like Sally, for instance, who tells tales. Or John, who pulls my hair.'

She began to feel excited. She picked up some of the fallen foxglove flowers.

'That pixie said I had better wear one on *each* thumb, to get more magic,' she thought. 'I think I'll take home *ten*, and wear one on each thumb, and on all eight of my fingers, too. That would surely make a very big wish indeed come true.'

She took about twelve foxglove flowers home. She remembered to take the fallen ones, of course. She saw a big bumble-bee in one of the flowers growing on a foxglove. He hummed loudly.

'Mmmmmmagic! Mmmmmmagic!'

'Well, I never heard a bee hum like that

SHE SAW A BIG BUMBLE-BEE IN ONE OF THE FLOWERS.

before!' said Jenny. 'He must have heard what the pixie said!'

She went home. She put the foxglove flowers beside her bed, ready to wear that night. She wondered how to keep them on all night.

'I'll have to go to sleep with my hands closed up,' she thought. 'Then the flowers will keep on. Or if they don't, I could slip elastic bands round. *Somehow* I'll make this foxglove magic work.'

She decided to begin the week exactly at half-past seven that night when she went to bed, and Mummy came to tuck her up.

'It's Thursday,' thought Jenny. 'So some-time next Thursday the wish should come true. I wonder what will happen? Will we be whisked off to the seaside? How surprised Daddy would be! Oh, dear – I do so hope everything goes well.'

That night Jenny began what she called her 'Magic Week.' She slipped the foxglove flowers on to her eight fingers and two thumbs, and closed her hands gently. Yes – she thought, the flowers would stay on all right.

'And I am making up my mind not to say or do a single unkind thing all the week,' she thought. 'Now – one, two, three – go!'

The week seemed very long indeed. Jenny wore the foxglove flowers each night, and they stayed on beautifully. She counted the days till Thursday.

'Tomorrow's Wednesday – then Thursday! And *sometime* on Thursday my wish will come true!'

Thursday came. When Jenny woke up she half thought she might find herself at the seaside already. But she was in her own bed. All that day she hoped and hoped that her wish would come true. Surely *somehow* they would all go to the seaside and have a lovely holiday.

But alas – when the night came nothing had

**SHE SLIPPED THE FOXGLOVE FLOWERS ON HER EIGHT
FINGERS AND TWO THUMBS.**

happened – nothing magic, anyway. Her wish
hadn't come true at all. Jenny was in tears.

'I haven't thought or said or done anything
unkind, I'm sure I haven't!' she said to herself.
'Oh, dear – doesn't foxglove magic work any
longer?'

When her mother came to tuck her up,
Jenny caught hold of her hand.

'Mummy – I want to ask you something.
Please answer truly. Mummy, can you possibly
think of a single unkind thing I've done this
week?'

'What a funny thing to ask me,' said her

mother. 'Let me thing. Well, yes, Jenny, I thought it rather unkind of you not to clean Bobby's bicycle after he had lent it to you. You made it all muddy.'

'Oh, *dear* – I didn't think!' said Jenny. 'I didn't *mean* to be unkind.'

'And I was rather surprised that you didn't take Granny a few flowers out of your garden when you knew she wasn't well,' said Mummy. 'When I told you I thought you should, you said you would, but you didn't.'

'I forgot,' groaned Jenny. 'I didn't think. Oh, Mummy, I didn't *mean* to be unkind.'

'No, I don't think you *ever* mean to be unkind, Jenny,' said Mummy. 'I think you really are a kind little girl. You just forget to think, sometimes – and *that's* unkind!'

Jenny looked so worried that Mummy laughed. 'You *asked* me to tell you, darling,' she said, 'or I wouldn't have done so. Nobody can be perfect, you know, so you needn't think too badly of yourself! You're much, much kinder than most children are. I'm really very proud of you.'

She kissed Jenny, turned out the light and left her. Jenny lay and thought. The week was up. Would it be any use starting another 'Magic Week'? It might be. This time she would be careful not to *forget* to be kind. Fancy that counting too! Oh, dear – was it possible to be perfectly and absolutely kind for a whole week?

Anyway, she tried again. She found some new fallen flowers in the foxglove glade, and began once more on Friday night. The days went by again – Saturday, Sunday, Monday – Tuesday, Wednesday, Thursday. Jenny anxiously asked herself if she had been horrid in any way.

'Have I? I've really tried so hard. Have I

SHE FOUND SOME NEW FALLEN FLOWERS.

spoilt the magic at all this week? Oh, dear – I shall never try again if I fail this time. Yes, I shall. I shan't give up.'

Friday came – the seventh day. Jenny took off the foxglove fingers. Now – would her wish come true this time? She dressed and went down to breakfast, wishing her wish with all her heart.

Daddy was already at the table, reading the paper. Mummy brought in the porridge. There came a noise from the hall and Daddy looked up.

'The letters,' he said. 'Get them, Jenny, will you?'

Jenny ran to get them. Four for Daddy – very dull-looking ones – and one for Mummy. Daddy opened his and tossed them aside. Mummy opened her one letter and began to read it. Then she suddenly gave a cry.

'Listen to this! It's from Auntie Adeline. Why, I haven't heard from her for years! And what *do* you think she says?'

'What?' asked Daddy and Jenny.

'Why, she says she is going to America for four weeks, and she wants to know if we'll go

MUMMY OPENED HER LETTER AND BEGAN TO READ IT.

and take care of her house for her,' said Mummy.

'Where does Great Aunt Adeline live?' asked Jenny.

'At the seaside,' said Mummy. 'A really lovely seaside place called Golden Sands. Would you believe it! We can have the house for four weeks for nothing! Oh, Daddy – and we thought we wouldn't be able to go away this summer!'

Jenny's eyes shone. 'Mummy! Can we go?'

'Of course,' said Daddy. 'I can only get two weeks off work, but I can come down for the week-ends as well – and you and Mummy can

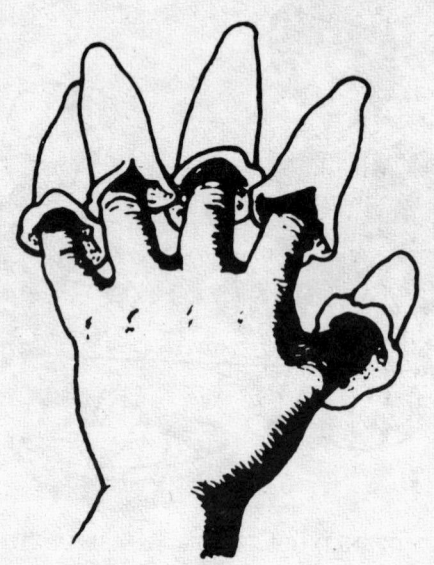

stay the whole of the time. It will be a wonderful holiday for you.'

Jenny felt in her pocket. She had the ten old foxglove flowers there. She squeezed them.

'Foxglove magic,' she thought. 'It's still there, then – the pixie was right. My wish has come true – and it really was a very big one!'

And now Jenny and her mother and father are all down at Golden Sands – and what a time they're having! I feel very glad about it.

Foxglove magic – well, you never know when you might like to try a little, do you?

You Can Draw An Aeroplane!

Would you like to be able to draw a really fine aeroplane?
You can quite easily draw one on the next page – I'll tell
you how.
Take your pencil and put the point on to Number 1. Now look
for Number 2, and draw a line to it from Number 1. Now go on
to Number 3 with your pencil, then to Number 4, and so on.
When you have come to Number 54, the last number of all,
you will see what a splendid aeroplane you have drawn.

ONE GOOD TURN DESERVES ANOTHER

THE mistletoe grew high up on a tall poplar tree. It was a queer plant. It didn't grow in the ground as most plants do. It liked to grow on the branch of a tree.

It grew there in a great thick tuft. It drank the poplar's sap, and used it to help itself to grow.

At Christmas time it was covered with pearly grey-green berries. A big bird saw them and came along to see if they were good to eat.

'Yes, eat me, eat me,' said the mistletoe. 'My berries are delicious. You will like them. Eat as many as you like, big bird. They are poisonous for children – but not for you!'

It was hungry weather. There were no other berries to be found. The bird ate the mistletoe berries greedily and enjoyed them.

'Thank you,' he said, when he had finished. 'You have done me a good turn. A very good turn. I was almost starving when I saw you. If ever I can do *you* a good turn, let me know, mistletoe.'

'Well – you can do me a good turn now, if you will,' said the mistletoe.

'What can I do?' asked the bird.

'Plant my seeds for me!' said the mistletoe. 'Will you do that?'

'But that's not a thing that I can do, not me!' said the bird. 'I don't know how to plant seeds.'

'All I want you to do is to go to that tree over there, sit on a branch and clean your beak,' said the mistletoe. 'Your beak is sticky, isn't it? It has some of my seeds still clinging to it. Go and wipe them off. That is the way you can plant my seeds for me!'

The big bird thought this sounded very queer, but he flew off to the nearby tree. It was true that his beak *was* sticky. He wiped it.

IT WAS TRUE THAT HIS BEAK WAS STICKY. HE WIPED IT.

Two or three seeds dropped off his beak and stuck to the branch. They were too sticky to fall from there to the ground.

'Well, I've done what you said!' cried the bird. 'But I'm sure I haven't planted your seeds!'

'Wait and see, just wait and see!' said the mistletoe.

One of the seeds rolled down to the underside of the branch. It clung there tightly. After a time the little seed put out a finger that went probing into the bark of the tree. It sank in. It sank itself so far that one day it reached the life-juice of the tree, its sap. And then it began to use it to help itself to grow – for sap makes all green things grow.

Two little sage-green leaves sprang from the seed. Then two more. Then yet another two – and when the big brown bird flew that way again some months later, what did he see?

He saw a fine little mistletoe plant, growing from the branch on which he had wiped his beak. 'You planted my seed for me! Thank you!' cried the mistletoe.

It's a strange little story, isn't it? Can you guess the name of the bird who plants the mistletoe seeds? Why – the mistle-thrush, of course!

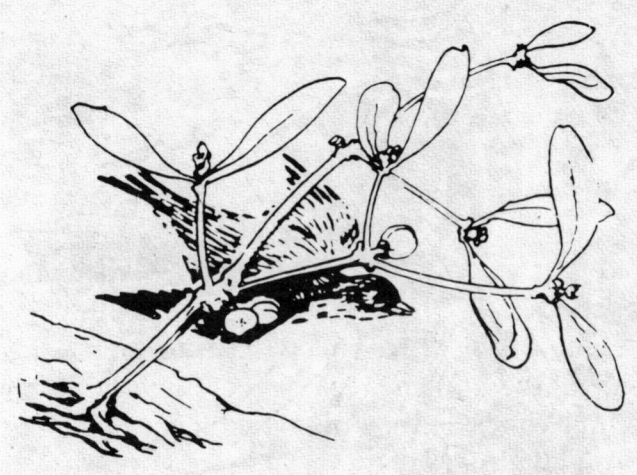

SEA SONG

I found a shell, a curly one,
Lying on the sand,
I picked it up and took it home,
Held tightly in my hand.

Mummy looked at it and then
She held it to my ear,
And from the shell there came a song,
Soft and sweet and clear!

I *was* surprised – I listened hard,
And it was really true;
If you can find a nice big shell,
You'll hear the singing too!

(*Yes, shells really do sing in your ear.
Next time you are by the
sea, find one, and listen.*)

JOAN MAKES A WINDMILL

'I SN'T it windy today?' said Joan. 'I'd like a paper windmill. I suppose you don't know how to make one, do you? It must be very, very difficult.'

'Oh no it isn't!' I said. 'Now let me see – what do we need? Some stiff paper, about eight or nine inches square. Your paint-box. Pencil and scissors. A good strong pin – and a stick which we can fasten the windmill to.'

'I can get all those!' cried Joan, and away she dashed. How quickly she could move when she wanted to!

We soon had a big piece of stiff paper on the table in front of us. I drew a line from the right-hand top corner to the left-hand bottom one, and another from the left-hand top corner to the right-hand bottom one, so that we had a big letter X on our paper. I put a little mark about three-quarters of the way up each line.

'Now you cut up the lines till you come to the little marks I have made, and then stop,' I said. 'That's right. Now, where's your paint-

box? Paint this side of the paper a bright red,
and the other side a bright yellow or blue –
whatever colour you like.'

Joan soon finished her painting. She painted
one side red and the other side green.

'Now comes the tricky bit,' I said. 'Where is
that pin? Here it is. Look, you must stick it
through one corner of your square. Now take
the next corner and put it under the pin and
stick it through – now the third corner in the
same way – and now the last one. The pin is
now through all the corners and all you have to
do is to press it down through the centre of the
paper . . .'

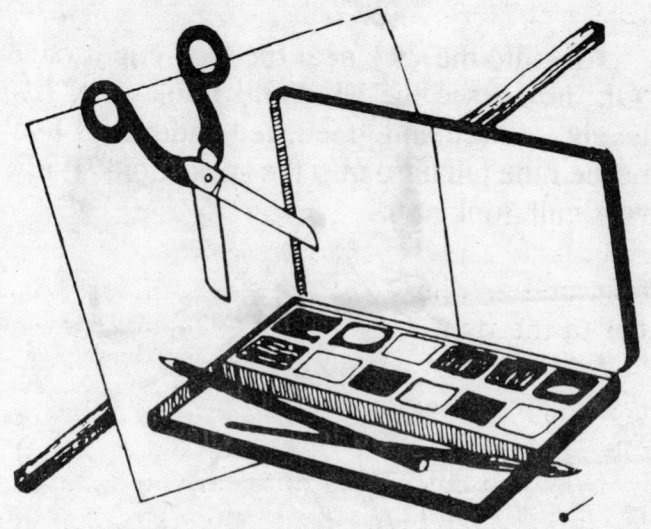

NOW, WHERE'S YOUR PAINT-BOX?

'LOOK AT MY WINDMILL, LOOK AT IT!'

'And into the stick near the top!' cried Joan. 'Oh, now I see the windmill! Look at it. It's lovely – all red and green, red and green! I've pushed the pin hard into the stick. Look at my windmill, look at it!'

And out she ran into the windy garden to see if the windmill blew round and round. Of course it did – and so will yours, too, if you make one! Why don't you?

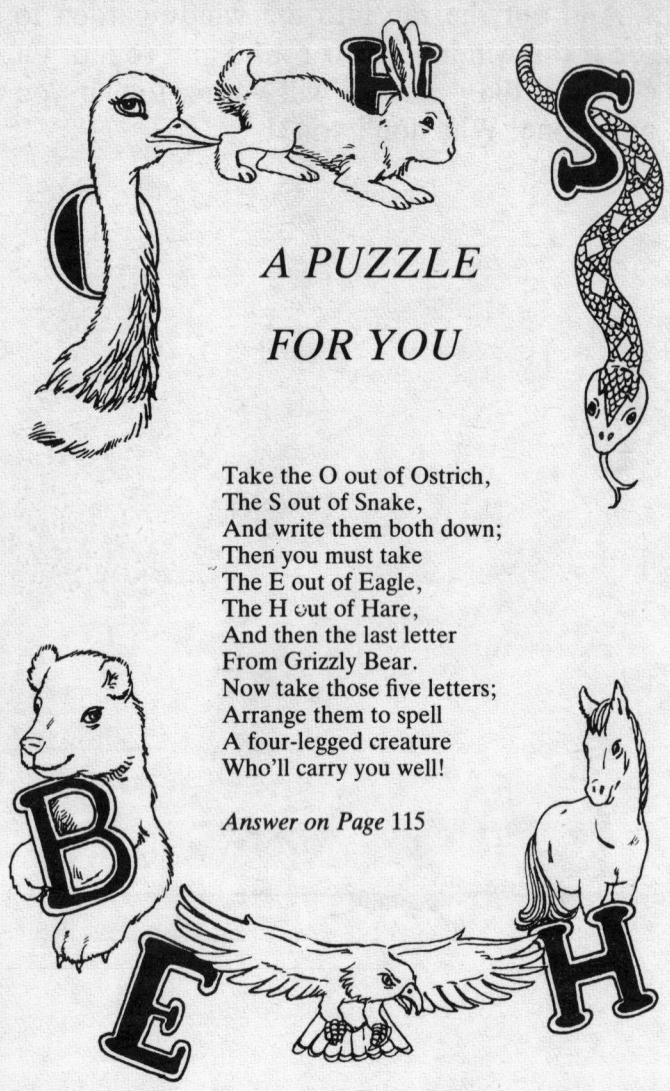

A PUZZLE
FOR YOU

Take the O out of Ostrich,
The S out of Snake,
And write them both down;
Then you must take
The E out of Eagle,
The H out of Hare,
And then the last letter
From Grizzly Bear.
Now take those five letters;
Arrange them to spell
A four-legged creature
Who'll carry you well!

Answer on Page 115

THEY WERE AFRAID OF DOGS

'COME for a walk, Sue and Jack!' shouted the boy over the road. 'No, thanks!' called back Sue at once.

'Why not?' shouted Harry. 'It's a lovely day. My dog's longing for a walk.'

'No, thanks!' called Jack, and he and Sue went in.

They were afraid of Spot, Harry's dog! He wasn't very big but he was very barky and boundy, and he *would* sniff round their ankles.

'He might snap,' said Sue. 'I don't like him!'

'You're silly!' said Mother. 'Spot always wags his tail when he sees you – he's just a jolly, friendly little dog. I do *wish* you wouldn't be so silly about dogs! You're silly about Wilfrid's dog too. The dogs to beware of are the ones that *don't* wag their tail when they see you! A tail-wag is a dog's way of smiling.'

Sue and Jack laughed – but it didn't make them want to go out with Harry. They were still afraid of Spot, even if he *did* smile with his tail whenever he saw them!

They went into the back garden to play. Soon somebody came and hammered at the back gate shouting to them. 'Hey, Sue, hey, Jack, come and do the shopping with me. I'm going down the town, and they say a circus is coming through the streets this morning.'

Jack ran and unlatched the gate. In came Wilfrid – and after him bounded his big, golden spaniel, his ears flopping up and down. Sue screamed and ran.

Rip the dog ran after her, thinking she was playing with him. She tripped and fell, and in a moment Rip was on top of her, barking and licking for all he was worth. Sue screamed so loudly that Mother came running at once.

But Wilfrid had already called Rip off, and was saying he was sorry that Sue was fright-

SHE SCREAMED AND RAN.

ened. 'Rip didn't mean it,' said Wilfrid. 'He was only playing. You needn't have screamed. You could just have pushed him off.'

Sue was very angry. Wilfrid was holding Rip by the collar, and she went up behind them.

Smack, smack, smack! She smacked Rip as hard as ever she could, and then Jack ran up and smacked him, too. He whined in pain.

'Don't! How horrid you are!' said Wilfrid, trying to get Rip out of the way of their smacks. 'I tell you, he didn't mean to frighten you. He was *playing*.'

Rip couldn't understand why he was being smacked so hard by these two people. He whined loudly and put his tail down miserably. Mother spoke sharply to Sue and Jack.

'Stop now. You are being unkind. You can't punish a dog simply because you are afraid of him. It's not his fault, it's yours!'

Wilfrid went off with Rip, very angry with Sue and Jack. 'Now you've offended Wilfrid, too,' said Mother. 'I really do think you're silly.'

She went indoors. Sue and Jack looked at each other gloomily.

'Now Mother's cross as well!' said Sue. 'Let's go out for a walk together, Jack – just the two of us. You take your bat and cricket ball and we'll go to that little place we know in the woods. Nobody will worry us there with their horrid dogs.'

So off they went to the woods. Jack carried his new bat and cricket ball. He was very proud of them indeed. He had just had them for his birthday, and they had cost a lot of money.

Sue took her new handbag with her. She had two shillings and threepence halfpenny in it. She was saving up for Mother's birthday.

They came to the little clearing in the woods. 'We'll have this tree to bat against,' said Jack, tossing Sue the ball. 'Oh, Butter-fingers! You always drop it!'

'Well, it's so *hard*,' said Sue, putting her handbag down beside a bush. 'Now I'll bowl. I bet I'll hit the tree and you'll be out!'

They played for some time, and Sue got Jack out, and then he bowled her out too. Sue suddenly gave a cry.

'Look! There's that nasty dog Rip again! He's sure to go for our ball!'

'I'LL BOWL. I BET I'LL HIT THE TREE AND YOU'LL BE OUT!'

But he didn't. He remembered the smacking that Sue and Jack had given him, and he sat down quietly, his tail quite still, without a single wag. He loved a game of ball, but these children didn't like him. They had smacked him. He wouldn't risk going for their ball in case they hit him again. He would just watch them play.

'Aha! Rip has remembered that we smacked him,' said Jack, pleased. 'Serves him right! He's afraid of *us* now!'

'*Bad* Rip, *naughty* dog, *bad* dog!' shouted Sue, feeling quite brave now that Rip was afraid.

Rip hung his head sadly. He got up with his tail between his legs and lay down under a bush, still watching the ball.

They went on playing, glad that Rip was too much afraid to come bounding up. Then they suddenly heard a loud voice, and looked round.

A big boy stood not far off, grinning. 'Hallo! Like to let me have a bat?'

'No,' said Jack, and frowned. He knew this boy. It was Will, a big, unkind fellow who loved to tease and chase the other children. He walked up to Jack. 'Come on,' he said, 'let me have a turn. Don't be a meanie. Come on.'

'We're just going home,' said Jack, hanging

on to his bat for all he was worth. Will would probably go off with it once he got it into his hands!

Sue had the ball. She was trembling. Oh, dear – this horrid, big boy – surely he wouldn't take Jack's new bat?

'Leave Jack alone!' she suddenly called, bravely, and Will turned and looked at her.

'Who's touching him?' he said. 'I only want to bat. Don't you cheek me! All right – if I can't bat, I'll bowl! Go on – give me the ball.'

He went up to Sue and wrenched the ball away from her. She began to cry. Will threw the ball hard at Jack who took a swipe at it with the bat to stop the ball from hitting him. It flew into the air and Will neatly caught it.

'Out!' he said. 'Come on, it's my turn to bat. I've caught you!' He walked up to Jack and snatched the bat from his hand. He looked at it closely.

'My word – this is a fine bat,' he said. 'I'll borrow it for today. We've got a match on with the boys in the next village. I'll take your bat and use it. It's better than mine!'

'Give me my bat and ball,' said Jack, angrily.

'Certainly not. You don't deserve them,' said Will. 'You wouldn't let me bat, so I'm going to borrow them both as a punishment to you for your meanness. You *may* get them back – and then again, you may not!'

He put the ball in his pocket, stuck the bat over his shoulder and began walking away. Suddenly he stopped. He had seen Sue's handbag on the grass nearby. He picked it up at once. He opened it and saw the money.

'No, no, don't take my money!' shouted Sue, in a panic at once. 'It's all I've got. It's for my mother's birthday.'

HE PUT THE BALL IN HIS POCKET, STUCK THE BAT OVER HIS SHOULDER AND BEGAN WALKING AWAY.

'Is it really?' said Will, mockingly. 'Funny now – *my* mother's got a birthday tomorrow – I'll buy her something with the money you've saved up! Here's your bag – catch!'

He slipped the money into his pocket and threw the bag to Sue. She was crying bitterly.

Rip was still under the bush, listening and watching in great surprise. Will hadn't seen him. Sue and Jack had forgotten all about him. But when he suddenly growled very loudly, they all jumped.

'That your dog?' said Will, suddenly seeing Rip's golden head under the bush. He didn't wait for an answer, but began walking away very quickly indeed. Rip slid out from under the bush, still growling. He was looking at the boy walking away between the trees. Sue was too upset even to feel afraid of the growling dog.

Jack looked at Rip, and knew that he was growling at the disappearing boy. 'Go for him!' he said suddenly. 'Get my bat and ball back! Go for him, Rip!'

And Rip went! He hadn't liked that boy, he hadn't liked his voice or his looks or his smell. He was very glad to rush after him, barking.

Will began to run – but Rip could run twice as fast. He soon caught up Will, and sprang at his legs. Down went the boy, yelling. Rip ran

'THAT YOUR DOG?' SAID WILL, SUDDENLY SEEING RIP'S
GOLDEN HEAD UNDER THE BUSH.

round him, growling and showing his teeth.
Whenever Will tried to get up Rip snapped at
him. He didn't even nip him, but Will was
terribly afraid he would. He sat there, not
daring to move.

Sue and Jack came up, panting. 'Now you
give me my bat and ball, and Sue's money,'
said Jack, fiercely. 'Go on! You're a bully,
that's what you are – but now this dog's
bullying *you*! Hand over our things.'

Will didn't. He looked at them and then at the dog. Should he hit Rip with the bat? Jack saw what he was thinking.

'If you hit him, he'll bite as sure as any-thing,' he said. 'Shall I tell him to nip you? Rip, you can n – '

But Will didn't wait for the rest of the sentence. He threw the bat and ball to Jack, and emptied Sue's money out of his pockets. He threw it towards her. Rip growled again.

'Call that dog off,' said Will, sulkily.

'Come here, Rip,' said Sue, and he came. Will got up and went off quickly, looking back every now and again to make sure that Rip was not following him.

Rip was standing by Sue and Jack, his head down and his tail between his legs. His big brown eyes looked solemnly at the ground.

'He's still afraid of us,' said Jack, ashamed. 'Fancy – we smacked him because he was playful – and now, although he's got back all our things for us, and is a very good, generous dog, he's still afraid of us. Rip!'

Rip looked up at the two children out of his mournful eyes. Then he lifted his tail and wagged it just a very little.

'He's giving us just a *tiny* smile,' said Sue. 'Oh, Rip – you're a very, very good dog! Don't be afraid of us any more, and we won't be

'OH, RIP – YOU'RE A VERY, VERY GOOD DOG!'

afraid of you either. Let's be friends.'

Rip barked joyfully. His tail went up at once. He leapt up at the two children, licking and pawing for all he was worth – just the thing they had always been afraid of any dog doing!

But somehow they didn't mind now. They let him lick them, and they patted him and then rolled the ball away for him to fetch. Soon he was fielding the ball marvellously and playing a very fine game of cricket indeed.

Wilfrid came to find him – and *how* astonished he was! 'Well! First you smack my dog, and then you play with him!' he said. 'I've a good mind not to let him play with you!'

But he did, of course, and he played, too. As for Rip, he was the very best fielder of them all.

'They ought to have him in test matches,' said Wilfrid, proudly. 'The other side would never get a run!'

Now they're all friends together, and I don't know who is most pleased about it. Rip, I think!

ANSWER TO A PUZZLE FOR YOU
Horse

Can You Find All These?

Look in my garden shed, and you'll see
A number of things beginning with P.
And just over there, beginning with S,
Two things together (they're easy to guess!).
Now three things beginning with B you will spot,
B.... and B... and B.... quite a lot!
And now look for something beginning with C,
And one little thing whose first letter is T.

Can you find them all?

(Answer on page 128)

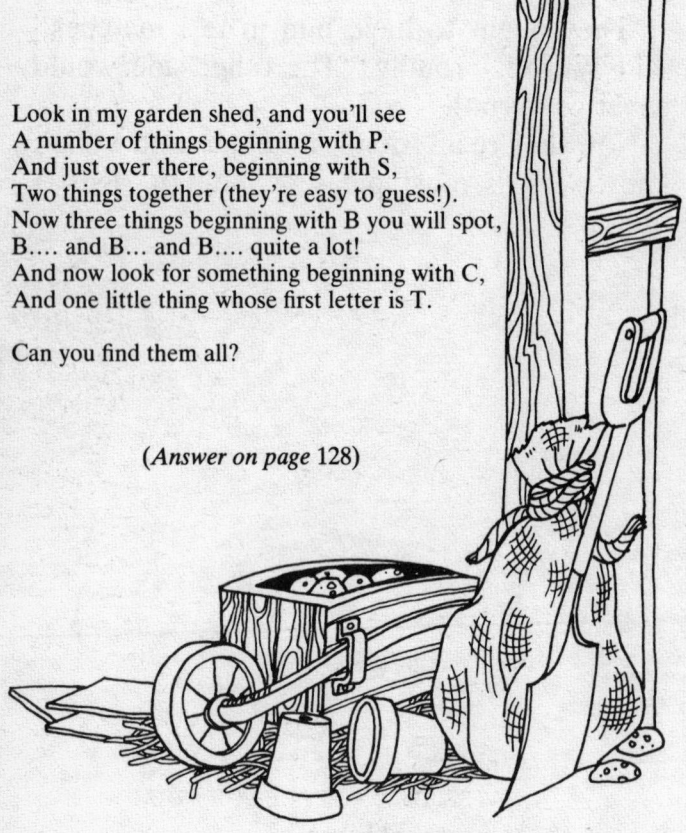

THE WONDERFUL
FISHERMAN

THERE was once a fisherman who went every Saturday afternoon to fish in the river near his home. He sat on a little stool, and threw his line into the water, with the bait on the hook at the end.

A little float that bobbed on the water told him when a fish bit, because then it would bob under in a very excited manner. But alas for the fisherman, he never seemed to be able to catch any fish at all!

'Yet there are plenty in the river,' he would say to himself. 'I can see them there!'

One day a brilliant blue, green and gold bird flashed past him and came to sit nearby. 'Hallo!' said the man, in surprise. 'What a beauty you are! Who are you?'

'I'm the king of all the fishers!' said the bird, opening its long, strong beak. 'Why do you sit here with a rod and a bit of line? That is not the way to catch fish!'

'Yes, it is,' said the man. 'Do you know a better way?'

He sat on a little stool, and threw his line into
the water.

'Oh *yes!*' said the bird. 'And I could teach
you a better way too. I am going to teach my
youngsters next week. Perhaps you would like
to watch me teaching them, and then maybe
you would know the right way to catch fish!'

'Bring your youngsters here then,' said the
man. 'I am always ready to learn! I shall be
surprised, though, if you are really king of the
fishers!'

The bird flew off. He went to a hole in the
river bank and there, at the end of it, was a

'I'M THE KING OF ALL THE FISHERS!' SAID THE BIRD.

smelly nest made of old fish-bones. In the hole were his four pretty children and his wife.

'Soon we must teach our children to fly and dive and fish,' said the bird. 'It is time they learnt.'

Well, the next Saturday, just as the fisherman sat down with his rod and line as usual, along came six brilliant streaks of colour, flashing through the air. They were the mother and father bird and their four children. They all perched on a branch that swung out over the river.

'Now watch, children!' said the father bird, and he dived headlong into the water at a fish he saw there. He came up with it wriggling in his beak. He sat himself on the bough and looked at his children in triumph.

'Your father must swallow the fish head-first, or it may stick in his throat,' said their mother. 'Watch him throw it up into the air to catch it the right way round for him to swallow.'

They watched. Their father threw the fish into the air and caught it so that he could swallow it head-first. It was gone!

HE THREW THE FISH INTO THE AIR AND CAUGHT IT.

'Now, watch for a fish to swim by, and then dive in, catch it, and come back to the branch,' said their mother.

But it was not as easy as it looked, and at first the young birds came back empty-beaked. Soon, though, they became quick at catching fish, and made a very good meal indeed.

'Now we'll all go home,' said the parent birds. 'Come along.'

They were flying off when the watching fisherman called to them. 'You certainly are wonderful at catching fish. What are your names?'

'Kingfishers!' they cried. 'Didn't you know *that*? If you fish the way we do, you'll soon catch plenty!'

But the poor old fisherman can't, can he?

'DIVE IN, CATCH ONE, AND COME BACK TO THE BRANCH.'

HAPPY NEW YEAR!

I T was the very last day of the Old Year, and the very last hour of it, too. The village clock had just struck eleven. Only one more hour to go until the first day of the New Year!

In the little village of Tippy-Top people were having parties. Tweaky, the pixie, had six friends to supper. Jimmy, the goblin, had five. Dame Patty-Pan had seven. Old Man Barley had goodness knows how many.

They were having a very merry time. 'And as soon as midnight comes, and the Old Year has gone, we will all go out and shout "Happy New Year" through the letter-box of every house,' said Old Man Barley. 'And what is more, we will take out drums and whistles to welcome the New Year in!'

Everyone was pleased to think of making such a noise. 'Nobody will be asleep, because everyone is having a party, or sitting up late,' said Dame Patty-Pan to her friends. 'They will like having Happy New Year shouted through their letter-boxes.'

Now Snoopy, the imp, knew quite well that many people would be at parties that night and would leave their cottages empty. He knew that Mother Clever-One would leave her house empty, too, to go to Dame Patty-Pan's party.

'And she's got more good spells and bottles of magic than anyone else in the world!' thought Snoopy. 'I'll sneak in through her window and snoop round to see what I can find. I'll be rich if I can slip away with some of her spells. My, she's got some beauties!'

So that night he crept out into the dark. He passed lighted windows and saw people having fun at parties. Snoopy hadn't been asked to any party at all. Nobody had wanted to invite him.

He came at last to Mother Clever-One's house. He slid quietly through the gate. He came to the window. Ah! It was open. Good!

He slipped in at the window and found himself in a dark room.

He drew the curtains behind him and lighted a candle. Mother Clever-One's black cat sat and blinked at him. 'Just say one single "mew" and I'll fill the bath and make you swim in it!' said Snoopy, fiercely. So the cat said nothing at all.

Snoopy began to hunt round. Ah! A bottle of Invisible Paint – and a box of yellow Growing Powder – and a tin of Good Dream Spells! Lovely! He set them all on a table together.

And then the village clock struck twelve. At once everyone's doors were flung open and out came the villagers. They ran down the street, calling through letter-boxes: 'A Happy New Year! Happy New Year!'

Somebody came to Mother Clever-One's house and yelled through the letter-box at the top of his voice:

'HAPPY NEW YEAR!'

Snoopy almost jumped out of his skin. He dropped the bottle he was holding. Before he could pick it up someone else came to the letter-box and yelled through it again:

'HAPPY NEW YEAR!'

Snoopy didn't know they were shouting that. He thought they were shouting 'FANCY YOU HERE! FANCY YOU HERE!'

'How do they know I'm here?' he thought in fright. 'Oh, dear – is it because I've got the candle alight?'

'HAPPY NEW YEAR!' That was someone else shouting through the letter-box. Snoopy blew out the candle in alarm. 'They shouted "Fancy you here" again,' he said to himself. 'Oh, dear – they *must* know I'm here then – what will they do to me?'

Well, the next thing he heard was the tremendous noise made by the beating of the drums and the blowing of the whistles to give the Old Year a send-off and the New Year a welcome. Bang-diddy-bang! Boom-boom-boom! Tee-tee-tiddley-tee! Boom-boom-BOOM!

MOTHER CLEVER-ONE'S CAT SAT AND BLINKED AT HIM.

'Off you go, off you go!' shouted the villagers to the Old Year, and then banged again to welcome in the New.

Snoopy heard 'Off you go, off you go!' and he felt certain they were shouting this at him. He was terrified at all the noise, too. Was a whole army of villagers marching against him?

He ran to the back door. He undid it with trembling fingers. The big black cat watched him. What was the matter with this nasty little creature now? Out went Snoopy into the night, fell into Mother Clever-One's duck-pond, waded out dripping wet, caught his clothes on the wire at the bottom of the garden, rolled down into the ditch there, and then fled for his life over the fields.

'Happy New Year! Happy New Year!' he heard as he went, and again he thought it was 'Fancy you here! Fancy you here!'

Ah! It was his own guilty mind that made him think that! Silly Snoopy to be so scared of good wishes! It served him right.

Nobody could imagine where or why Snoopy had gone when they found his cottage empty the next day. 'Well – it's good riddance to bad rubbish, that's all I can say,' said Mother Clever-One. 'He never was any good, that's certain!'

He never will be, either – and when the next

New Year comes, what a shock he'll get again. Happy New Year! What will he think it is next time?